Scottish Fairy Tales

Born into a Lanarkshire police family in 1913, Donald Grant Campbell served for over 30 years in the Perth and Kinross Constabulary and thereafter in the Civil Service.

A life-long interest in the history of Scotland, and the consciousness that the old traditions were passing, led him to collect legendary tales both verbal and written. In this collection of 12, there are enchanted knights, changelings, ghostly pipers, mermen and fairies, both good and bad.

These traditional stories come from all parts of Scotland, where even today lonely places can still be found, where one can imagine their settings – when viewing the mountains in the moonlight or sitting in the sun by a quiet stream – from Canonbie near the English border to Muckle Flugga in the north of Shetland.

D1430436

Grant Campbell

Scottish Fairy Tales

Illustrated by Jane Bottomley

A Piccolo Original
Piccolo Books

First published 1980 by Pan Books Ltd,
Cavaye Place, London SW10 9PG
This new edition published 1986.
9 8 7 6 5 4
© Grant Campbell 1980
Illustrations © James Bottomley 1980
ISBN 0 330 26136 3
Set, printed and bound in Great Britain by
Cox & Wyman Ltd, Reading

to Nan

Contents

The piper of Badenoch 9

The seal-catcher 17

The meal mill of Eathie 25

The Laird o' Co 31

The blacksmith and the fairies 37

The fox and the wolf 43

The elfin knight 51

The brownie and the green slippers 61

Thomas the Rhymer 65

The Dwarfie Stone 75

Habetrot the spinstress 89

The page boy and the silver goblet 101

The piper of Badenoch

Once upon a time in the district of Inverness-shire known as Badenoch there was a famous piper called Iain who played the bagpipes more skilfully than any piper had ever done before. When he played the rousing marches of Scotland the young men who heard him were filled with determination to be brave in battle and to perform great deeds of daring; while the old men dreamt of past splendours and the fame they had gained on the battlefields. If he played soft music of the heart the young girls would sigh for they knew not what while the old women would mourn for their lost youth. When he played the gay lilting reels of Scotland the feet of the young men and girls were set dancing and twirling. The hands of the old men and women were set clapping and there would be laughter and happiness, the cares and worries of the world forgotten.

It is not surprising, then, that Iain was always in demand at weddings or at any occasion when there was something to celebrate and the people wished to dance and make merry. Neither was it surprising that the fairies should soon come to hear of his great skill. It is well known that certain fairies, however enchanting their own music may be, dearly love to hear music that is played by mortal men, especially if that music is played on the bagpipes. The Badenoch fairies planned to capture Iain so that he might play to them in their underground fairy halls.

One day, Iain was invited to play at the wedding of the laird's daughter. It was a big wedding and nearly everyone from miles around attended. When the ceremony was over and the feasting and drinking had begun, Iain was asked to play. Such was his skill that day it made even old folk get to their feet and join in the dancing. On and on played Iain, and whenever he stopped to rest there were shouts and cries for: 'More music, Iain, more music.' He continued to play into the night until at last even the liveliest of the dancers was too tired to ask for more. Iain, who was also worn out, put his bagpipes into his shoulder bag and set out on his long walk home to Ruthven.

His journey was by way of the Minigaig Pass which in winter has claimed the death of many a traveller. Iain was so tired that halfway home he was forced to rest. He lay on a grassy hillock with his shoulder bag underneath his head and fell asleep. In the grey light of dawn it was there that the fairies found him and by pulling at his nose the little people aroused him from his sleep. Had Iain not been too tired to recognize the danger, he would have jumped to his feet and raced away to the safety of his home. As it was, he was flattered that the fairies should bother with him and he answered their questions cheerfully.

'Are you Iain the Piper?' asked one little man.

'Aye, that I am,' replied Iain.

'Will you rest with us for an hour or so?' asked a little lady, whose green dress was the colour of wet moss.

'Aye, thank you kindly, that I will do,' replied Iain.

'And will you come to our fairy halls underground?' asked another little man.

Iain hesitated for a moment and then agreed to go with them. It was not often that a human had such a chance offered to him and it would be a fine story to tell his wife when he saw her later in the day. He let the fairies lead him to a nearby hillock, at the side of which was a cave entrance. The fairies all poured through this opening followed by Iain carrying his precious bagpipes. They travelled down a long dark passage until they reached a huge hall which was lit by a thousand fairy candles casting shadows among the chattering and laughing fairies. Some of them were eating from plates of gold and drinking out of silver goblets while the rest danced and sang to the music of their own fairy piper.

As soon as Iain stepped into the hall his weariness left him. He felt gay and carefree. When asked if he would play his bagpipes for the fairy company, he readily agreed. He played as one bewitched and the fairies were delighted with him. They had never heard music like this before and in turn Iain had never seen dancing like theirs before. The faster he played the faster they danced. Their feet seemed scarcely to touch the ground and their flimsy green garments floating through the hall reminded Iain of mist and clouds floating over the mountains. He played for what he thought was an hour or two, but in fairyland time has no meaning. Above ground, his wife waited anxiously for him to return home. When Iain had not appeared by the next day she went to the laird whose daughter had been married on the day of his disappearance.

'Where is Iain, my husband?' she asked. She was assured that her husband had left to go home in the early morning after the wedding party broke up. A search party was organized and Iain's friends and family looked for him high and low but he was nowhere to be found. The months and years went by but still there was no news of him. People began to forget Iain the Piper, and his wife married again. That might have been the end of it had it not been for an old nurse called Meg who was a friend of the fairies and very occasionally they sent to her for help in curing sickness which the fairy herbs were unable to cure.

One day, years after Iain's disappearance, a fairy messenger visited Meg and begged her to come below ground where a fairy baby lay sick and ailing. Meg put on her bonnet and set out with the messenger. She reached the hillock and went along the dark passage into the fairy hall where she was surprised to see Iain playing his bagpipes. Before she had a chance to speak to him she was led to another hall where she tended to the baby. She wondered if it was really Iain she had seen. On her way back through the hall where the piper was playing she spoke to him, saying: 'Is it Iain the Piper then?'

'Aye,' he replied, 'but what is that to you?'

'I remember you,' said Meg. 'When I was a young girl I remember going to the wedding of the laird's daughter where you played. I have never forgotten your music.' Iain gazed at the old woman before him. She was bent with rheumatism, her face was wrinkled, her hair was white.

Iain shook his head. 'When you were a young girl! I don't understand.'

'You have been here a long time, Iain the Piper,' said Meg. 'I recall that you disappeared soon after the wedding I speak of.'

'That was last night,' cried Iain. 'Last night the fairies asked me to rest here for an hour after the wedding. Away with you, woman, you are mad and know not what you say.'

'Remember Angus the shepherd?' asked Meg. 'He was young when you were young. Last winter they buried him and his grandchildren came to the funeral. Remember the woodcutter's little boy whom you used to take fishing on the Spey? His younger son was married in the Kirk of Alvie last spring. Remember Farmer Grant's babe? You played at her christening, didn't you? Well, you weren't there to play at her firstborn's christening last week.'

Iain shook his head in confusion, refusing to believe what the old woman told him. He picked up his pipes and began to play with great fury, as if by doing so he could forget the unpleasant news he had just heard. Meg hurried home and soon the great news she had brought with her was round the district. *Iain the Piper is in fairyland.* The question was how to get him out of there. Nearby there lived a wise man, who, it was said, had even greater power than the fairies. As Meg was the only person to have set eyes on Iain in his fairy surroundings she was appointed by the villagers to approach the wise man.

She asked the wise man: 'How may we get the piper out of fairyland?' At first there was no reply. The wise man spent some time bent over his large books of magic. At last he seemed to have found what he wanted. He said: 'Take me to the hillock on the Minigaig where lies the entrance to the fairy hall you tell me about.'

Meg led the wise man to the place.

Followed by the curious villagers, the wise man stayed at the entrance all night, sometimes muttering words of magic, sometimes consulting his books while nodding and mumbling to himself. As the cock crowed at the first light the wise man lifted up his arms and there came a faint sound of bagpipe music from the cave entrance. As the villagers watched, the music gradually swelled until out of the cave marched Iain playing his skirling pipes. There was a great gasp from the crowd and some of the old men who had known Iain in the years gone by went forward to greet him. Iain appeared to be lost and dazed. He was unable to recognize his old friends. One of his old friends took him to his house where he gave him food and put him to bed. Iain spoke to no one but lay quietly in the bed with his bagpipes by his side and his face turned to the wall. He stayed thus for many weeks in the friend's house until one evening when he had been left alone for an hour or two he rose from the bed, took up his bagpipes, and marched away towards the hillock on the Minigaig Pass.

No one ever saw him again. It seemed that his only happiness was with the fairies. In dark Glen Feshie, Comyn's Road and Minigaig Pass it is said that the music of a ghost piper can still be heard on a calm clear day.

The seal-catcher

Once upon a time there was a man who lived near John o' Groats' house in the far north of Scotland and made a living by catching seals and selling their skins. It was said that some of the larger seals were actually mermen or merwomen who were able to change into human beings. However, they had to be careful when discarding their seal-like skins which they usually hid among the rocks. If the discarded skin was lost or carried away they could never return to live in the sea. The seal-catcher did not believe in mermen or merwomen – to him they were merely larger seals which he was anxious to catch as their skins were more valuable.

It came about one day that the seal-catcher was searching the rocky shore near his house where the seals often came to sleep and bask in the sunshine. It was not difficult to come quietly up behind and kill them with a hunting knife. He thus managed to creep up on one seal and stabbed it with his knife. But his aim was poor, the seal woke up, gave a loud cry of pain, slipped off the rock and disappeared into the sea with the hunting knife stuck in its back. The seal-catcher was annoyed by the loss of his good hunting knife and decided to go home for his dinner.

On his way home he met a horseman riding a large grey horse. The rider was tall and strange-looking and he appeared to be interested in the seal-catcher as he stopped and asked him what his trade was. On hearing that he was a seal-catcher the strange horseman immediately ordered a large number of sealskins. The catcher was very pleased with the order which would mean a large sum of money for him. The horseman then made a condition that the skins must be delivered that evening without fail.

'I cannot do it,' the catcher said in a disappointed voice, 'for I have lost my knife and I disturbed the seals this morning. They will not return to the rocks until tomorrow morning.'

'I can take you to a place where there are many seals and I will supply you with a new knife,' answered the stranger, 'if you will mount behind on my horse and come with me.'

The seal-catcher, who was very greedy for money, agreed to the suggestion made by the horseman. He climbed up behind the rider and off they went flying like the wind until they came to the edge of a great precipice, the face of which went straight down to the sea. The horseman stopped at the edge and told the seal-catcher to dismount.

He then took a large sealskin from his saddle bag and instructed the seal-catcher to put the skin over his shoulders before looking over the edge of the cliff to see if there were any seals lying on the rocks below. The stranger explained that the seals would not take fright if he approached them with the skin over his shoulders. The seal-catcher looked cautiously over the edge but to his astonishment he saw no rocks below, only the clear blue sea which came right up to the foot of the cliff.

'Where are the seals you spoke of?' he asked anxiously,

wishing now that he had never agreed to accompany the horseman.

'You will see presently,' answered the stranger who was attending to his horse.

Standing with the sealskin over his shoulders the seal-catcher was by now very frightened. Not without reason, for suddenly the stranger pushed against his shoulder and he felt himself falling over the cliff and with a great splash he landed in the sea. He thought that he would be drowned and wondered why the stranger had pushed him over. To his astonishment, instead of being choked by the sea water he was able to breathe quite easily. He also saw that the stranger was close by his side in the water.

They both seemed to be sinking fast to the bottom of the sea. Down and down they went until at last they came to a huge door with seaweed hanging all around. The door opened of its own accord and when they entered they found themselves in a huge cavern, the floor of which was covered with yellow sand and the walls studded with all kinds of seashells which made them shine like mirrors. The huge door seemed to have shut out the sea water.

The large cavern was crowded with seals and when the seal-catcher turned to his companion the horseman to ask for an explanation he was aghast to find that he had taken on the form of a large seal. He was still more upset when he caught sight of himself in the mirror-like walls for he also had been transformed into a seal with the same skin which the stranger had asked him to put over his shoulders.

'What has happened to me?' he asked himself. 'A spell

has been laid on me by the stranger and I will remain a seal for the rest of my life.'

At first none of the creatures paid any attention to him. For some reason or other they all seemed to be very sad and moved about gently over the sand floor muttering mournfully to one another. Some were sitting about weeping and wiping the tears from their eyes with their soft furry fins. Presently they began to notice him and started whispering among themselves. At the same time the horseman-turned-seal, went to the end of the cavern and disappeared through a door set in the wall. When he returned he was carrying a large knife.

'Did you ever see this before?' he asked the unfortunate seal-catcher, who at once recognized his own hunting knife.

Seeing the knife he grew afraid that the seals would take revenge on him for wounding their companion. He begged for mercy. But instead of doing him any harm they crowded round rubbing their soft dog-like noses against his fur to show their sympathy. They told him that he would not be punished and that they would love him always if only he would do what was to be asked of him.

'Tell me what it is,' said the seal-catcher, 'and I will do it if it lies within my power.'

'Follow me,' answered his guide, leading the way through the door at the end of the cavern.

The seal-catcher was then taken to a small cave where a great brown seal with a gaping knife-wound on its side was lying on a bed of seaweed.

'That is my father,' said his guide, 'whom you wounded this morning, thinking that he was one of the common seals who live in the sea instead of a merman who has the same speech and understanding as yourself. I brought you here to bind his wound for no other hand can heal him.'

'I have no doctor's skill in the art of healing,' said the seal-catcher, who was anxious to help the creature, 'but I will bind up the wound as best I can and I am very sorry that it was my hand that caused it.' He went over to the seaweed bed and, stooping over the wounded merman, set to work as well as he could. The touch of his hands, which were in fact fins, appeared to work like magic for he had no sooner finished than the wound seemed to heal up with only a scar to be seen. The old seal then rose up as well as ever.

There was great rejoicing in the Palace of the Seals. They laughed and embraced each other in their strange way, crowding around their comrade who had been injured and rubbing their noses against his to show their delight. Meanwhile the seal-catcher stood aside in a corner with his mind filled with dark thoughts. He knew that the seals did not intend to kill him but he did not relish the prospect of spending the rest of his life in the form of a seal deep down in the sea.

Presently his guide approached and said: 'Now you are free to return home to your wife and children. I will take you back to them, but only on one condition.'

'What is the condition?' asked the seal-catcher eagerly. He was overjoyed to think that he might be restored safely to his family.

'You must take a solemn oath never to wound a seal again.'

'That I will do gladly,' replied the seal-catcher, for, although it meant giving up his only means of livelihood, he considered that if he could only regain his proper shape he would be able to work at some other job. He took the required oath, holding up his fin as he spoke and all the other seals crowded round to witness the oath-taking. A great sigh of relief went through the cavern when the words were spoken for the seals knew that he was the best seal-catcher in the north of Scotland.

After taking the oath he bade farewell to the strange company and, accompanied by his guide, he went through the huge doors, then up and up through the sea until they emerged into the bright sunlight. With one great spring they both reached the top of the cliff where the large grey horse still patiently waited. As they sprang up from the sea their strange seal disguise dropped off and at the clifftop they were both again in human form. A plainly dressed seal-catcher and a tall well-dressed gentleman in riding clothes.

'Get up behind me,' said the gentleman. The seal-catcher mounted behind and took a tight hold of his companion's coat. The bridle was shaken and the horse galloped off. It was not long before the seal-catcher found himself standing safely at his own garden gate. He then held out his hand to say 'Goodbye' to the horseman, but as he did so the stranger pulled out a large bag of gold from his saddle bag and handed it over to the seal-catcher.

'You have done your part, we must do ours,' he said. 'Men will never say that we took away an honest man's living without making sure that he will live in comfort for the rest of his days.' The man and horse then sped off towards the sea.

When the seal-catcher carried the bag into his cottage and turned out the gold he found that what the stranger had said was true. He remained a rich man for the rest of his life and always tried to protect the seals from the local hunters.

The meal mill of Eathie

Many years ago near Rosemarkie by the side of a fast-flowing burn stood a famous meal mill which used the burn water to turn the large mill wheel outside. One night the miller was working late when he heard the sound of horses and the rattling of carts outside. He was surprised to hear horses and carts at such a late hour so he went to the door to find out who the late callers might be.

On looking out he saw a long line of small carts drawn by small shaggy ponies of every colour. The drivers were slim, unearthly creatures about three feet in height dressed in dark grey with red caps. This strange caravan seemed to have come out of a square opening in the cliff face opposite the mill. The creatures appeared to be as much frightened at seeing the miller at the door as he was at seeing them. One of them uttered a shrill scream and almost immediately they all disappeared into the opening on the cliff face which closed after them.

It happened that Tam McKechan, a drover, heard about the mysterious creatures seen by the miller. As a drover, Tam travelled with the small, hardy breed of black cattle to the markets at Crieff and Falkirk. His only protection was his dirk concealed in the folds of his plaid and the stout stick with which he directed the movements of the cattle through the dangerous country. Tam laughed at the story told by the miller and volunteered to spend a night at the mill with only his bagpipes as company.

It was also arranged that a young farmer named Jock Hossack should also spend the night at the mill as company for the drover but Tam would not agree. The young farmer advised Tam not to go into the mill alone. 'No. I must go alone and keep my good music for the little people. I will not flinch now, but you can come with me to the burn edge and return early in the morning if you wish,' said Tam.

The miller and Jock returned early next morning to find the mill door open but all was silent within. There was no trace of Tam except for an overturned stool and one of the drones of Tam's bagpipes lying among the ashes in the mill fireplace. Weeks passed and still nothing was heard of Tam.

Jock Hossack resolved to try and clear up the mystery and so he went again to the mill to stay the night. For the first few hours the only sound heard was the rush of the stream as it swept past the mill wheel. He piled wood on the fire which made a cheerful glow. Jock then started to prepare a meal by roasting a duck suspended over the fire and nearly forgot all about the fairies. The duck was nearly ready for eating with the drippings sputtering among the embers when he heard a burst of music from outside. 'That must be Tam's pipes,' said Jock, and he went to a window to look out. He saw that on a level green by the waterside a crowd of small creatures were gathered; some were dancing to music which was certainly not that of bagpipes.

Jock decided to wait inside and resumed his seat at the fireside but facing the closed door which was firmly bolted. He had just sat down when he heard a soft tap at the door, and shortly after a second and a third. Jock sat still and turned round to see if the duck was fully cooked. He had no wish for visitors and was determined to admit none. But when he looked back at the door he was surprised to see that, though firmly bolted, it was opening slowly and there entered one of the strangest-looking creatures he had ever seen. The figure was that of a man, but it was little more than three feet in height; and though the face was as sallow and wrinkled as that of a person of eighty, the eyes had a roguish sparkle and the limbs appeared to be very active.

'What is your name, man?' said the little fellow.

'Mysel an' Mysel' (myself), said Jock.

'Ah, Mysel an' Mysel,' rejoined the creature, 'and what is that you have got there, Mysel an' Mysel?' touching the duck with its forefinger and then transferring part of the scalding gravy on to the cheek of Jock. The creature asked the same question again and dabbed Jock's other cheek with a larger and more scalding application of gravy.

'What is it?' he exclaimed, losing in his anger all thought of consequences, and taking the duck from the iron on which it hung he dashed it across the face of the visitor, remarking, 'It's that.' The little creature, blinded and burned, screamed out in pain and terror.

The music outside ceased and Jock had barely time to cover the fire with fresh fuel, which in a few seconds reduced the room to almost total darkness, when the crowd outside came swarming like bees to every door and window of the mill.

'Who did it, Sanachy – who did it?' was the query of a hundred voices.

'Oh, it was Mysel an' Mysel,' said the creature.

'And if it was yoursel and yoursel, who, poor Sanachy,' replied his companions, 'can help that?' However, they still clustered round the mill; the flames began to rise from the fire and Jock Hossack had just given himself up for lost when a cock crowed outside the building. He was aware of a sudden breeze and sounds from outside for a few seconds, then he found himself alone once again with the roast duck still hot lying at his feet. Jock stayed no longer at the mill as dawn was breaking, and in time he married the sister of the missing drover, who never returned to Rosemarkie.

The Laird o' Co

One fine summer morning the Marquess of Ailsa, laird of
Culzean, was walking on the green turf outside his castle
overlooking the Firth of Clyde. The local people of the
Ayrshire coast always called him the Laird o' Co because
of the co's or caves found in the old red sandstone cliffs on
which his castle stood.

This laird we speak of lived many years ago before the
present castle was built. He was a kind and courteous
person, always interested in the affairs of the poor people
among his neighbours, willing to help in times of trouble,
and to listen to the many tales of woe.

On this summer morning a little boy came across the
green carrying a small can in his hand. He saluted the
laird and asked if he might have permission to go into the
castle and beg some ale for his sick mother. The laird
gave his consent at once and, patting the boy on the head,
told him to go direct to the kitchen of the castle and ask
for the butler. He was instructed to tell the butler that the
laird had given orders that the can carried by the boy was
to be filled with the very best ale that was in the cellar.

Away the boy went and found the old butler who had
been in the service of the laird for many years. After listen-
ing to the message given by the boy he took him down into
the cellar and started to carry out his master's orders.
There was one cask of particularly fine ale which was kept

31

for the laird's own use. This cask had been in use for some time and was then only about half full.

'I will fill the boy's can out of this,' thought the old butler to himself. 'The ale is both nourishing and light; the very thing for sick folk.' So, taking the can from the boy, he proceeded to draw the ale. He was then astonished to find that although the ale flowed freely enough from the cask, the little can, which could have held no more than two pints, remained always just half-filled.

The ale poured into the can in a clear amber stream until the big cask was empty and still the boy's can remained only half full. The butler was amazed. He looked into the cask and then into the can. He also examined the floor of the cellar at his feet to see if the ale had not spilt away. No, the floor was dry and the ale had not disappeared in that way.

'The can must have been bewitched!' thought the old man who became afraid. The hair round the bald patch on the top of his head stood up like hedgehog quills, for if there was anything on earth of which he had a mortal fear it was warlocks and witches. 'I am not going to broach another cask,' he said, handing back the half-filled can to the little boy. 'You must go home with your can half-filled as the laird's ale is too good to be wasted,' said the old butler.

The little boy did not agree. A promise is a promise and the laird had both promised and sent orders to the butler that the can was to be filled and he would not go home to his mother until it was filled. His plea was in vain, the old butler first argued and then became angry but the boy would not leave the cellar. The laird had said that he was

to get the can filled with ale and filled it must be.

At last, the butler left the boy standing in the cellar and hurried off to find the laird and tell him that the can carried by the boy was bewitched as it had swallowed up half a cask of ale and then was only half full. He asked the laird to go down to the cellar and order the boy to leave the castle.

'Not I,' said the genial laird, 'for the little fellow is quite right. I promised that he should have his can full of ale to take home to his sick mother and he shall have it if it takes all the casks in my cellar to fill it. So back to the cellar, butler, and open another cask.'

The butler dared not disobey; so he reluctantly retraced his steps, shaking his head sadly. It seemed to him that not only the boy with the can but his master was also bewitched. When he returned to the cellar he found the boy waiting patiently beside the empty ale cask. Without saying a word, the butler took the half-empty can and broached another cask of the fine ale. If he had been amazed before, the butler was now even more astonished for hardly a drop or two had fallen from the tap of the new cask into the can when it was full to the brim.

'Take it, laddie, and away you go,' he said, glad to have the can taken away. The boy immediately took the can and thanked the old butler for all his trouble. The boy then departed and he made no mention of the old man having been so uncivil to him at the first cask. The butler was ashamed of his anger and he made inquiries throughout the district but he was unable to trace the boy. No one knew anything about him or about his sick mother.

Many years passed and the Laird o' Co was captured

while serving with an army in France. As a prisoner condemned to death he was shut up in a dark, damp dungeon. Alone in a foreign country without friends to help him, escape from the dungeon seemed impossible. On the night before his execution he was sitting in the dungeon thinking of his wife and children in faraway Ayrshire. The future of his home was clearly in his mind. He was thinking of the early-morning walks on the green turf beside the castle walls, when suddenly the same little boy of many years ago, carrying a can and begging for ale to help his sick mother, appeared before him.

The laird had forgotten all about the boy but the vision was so clear that he felt almost as if the years had rolled back and a familiar scene was being enacted again. He rubbed his eyes to clear the vision but as he did so the heavy studded door of the dungeon slowly opened and there on the threshold stood the same little boy who appeared not a day older. He had his left forefinger held to his lips and there was a smile upon his face. 'Laird o' Co, Rise and go,' he whispered, beckoning the laird to follow him. Needless to say, the laird did so, too amazed to think of asking any questions.

Through the dark passages of the prison went the little boy, the laird following close at his heels. Whenever the boy came to a locked door it opened at his touch and they were soon safely outside the prison walls. The overjoyed laird was about to thank the boy, but before he could do so the boy said: 'Get on my back for you are not safe until you are out of this country.' The laird wondered how a small boy would be able to carry him on his back but he did as he was bid. The boy did not appear to have any trouble in bearing the weight of the man. As soon as the laird was comfortably seated they set off over land and sea, never stopping until the dawn of day when the boy set him down on the same green turf outside the Castle of Culzean where they had first met many years before.

The boy then laid his little hand on the laird's big right hand and said:

'One good turn deserves another. Take your liberty for being so kind to my old mother.'

The boy immediately vanished and was never seen again about the Carrick shore.

The blacksmith and
the fairies

Years ago in Crossbrig there lived a blacksmith named MacEachern who had an only child, a boy of about fourteen years of age, who was always cheerful, strong and healthy until he suddenly became very ill. The boy was confined to bed, but no one could tell what was the matter with him. He appeared to be wasting away fast, getting thin, old and yellow, and his father and all his friends were afraid that he would not recover.

At last, one day, after the boy had been lying in this condition for a long time, getting neither better nor worse, always confined to bed, but with an extraordinary appetite, the smith was standing looking into the forge fire thinking sadly about his boy when he was surprised to see an old man walk into the smithy. The old man was well known to the smith and people round about for his knowledge of out-of-the-way things and happenings. The smith decided to tell the old man the story of his son's illness which had clouded his life and was causing him great grief.

The old man looked grave as he listened; and after sitting a long time on the smithy anvil pondering over all he had heard, he gave his opinion, saying: 'It is not your son you have. The boy has been carried away by the fairy people and they have left in his place a dangerous cast-out goblin who has been changed to look like your son.'

'Alas, and what then am I to do?' said the smith. 'How am I ever to see my own son again?'

'I will tell you how,' answered the old man. 'But, first, to make sure that it is *not* your own son you have, take as many empty eggshells as you can find, go with them into the bedroom, spread them out carefully before his sight, then proceed to draw water with them, carrying them two by two in your hands as if they were a great weight. Then, when all are full, arrange them round the fireplace with every sign of earnestness.'

That afternoon the smith accordingly gathered as many broken eggshells as he could get, went into the bedroom and proceeded to carry out all the instructions given by the old man.

He had not been long at work before there arose from the bed a shout of laughter and the voice of the seemingly sick boy exclaimed: 'I am now 800 years of age and I have never seen the like of that before.'

The smith returned to the smithy workshop where the old man was waiting and he told him of what had happened.

'Well, now,' said the old man, 'did I not tell you that it was not your son you have been looking after; your son is a captive in the fairy hill. Get rid of the intruder as soon as possible and I think I can promise you your own son. You must heap fresh fuel on the fire before the bed on which the stranger is lying so that the room becomes very hot. He will then ask you why you make the fire so hot. Answer him at once saying that he will find out presently, then pull him from the bed towards the fire. If it is your own son he will call out for you to save him, but if not, this thing will fly away up the chimney before the flames can touch him.'

The smith again followed the old man's instructions; he made up a large fire, answered the question put to him as he had been instructed, and seizing the intruder flung him towards the fire. The intruder gave a loud scream of fright and immediately seemed to vanish up the chimney before the flames could reach him.

Afterwards, the old man told him that on a certain night the entrance to the fairy hill where his son might be would be open. On that night the smith was to proceed to the hill carrying his Bible, his dirk and a crowing cock. He was also told by the old man that he would hear singing and dancing together with much merriment going on but he was to advance into the hill boldly; the Bible he carried would be a certain safeguard to him against any danger from the fairies. On entering the hill he was to stick the dirk in the threshold to prevent the hill from closing in after him. He was further instructed that he would come to a large compartment where he would probably see his son working as a blacksmith. If questioned by any fairy guard he had to say that he had come to seek his son and would not leave without him.

Not long after he had received his instructions the smith made his way in moonlight to the hill. As he approached he saw a light on the hill where he had never seen a light before. The sound of piping, dancing and merriment reached the anxious father on the night wind. Overcoming every fear, the smith carried on to an open cave-like threshold. He stuck his dirk into the soft earth at the side and entered. Protected by the Bible he carried, the

fairies could not touch him but they asked with apparent displeasure what he wanted by entering into their dwelling place. He answered: 'I want my son whom I see working at your forge and I will not leave without him.'

On hearing this the whole company of fairies started laughing. The loud sound of laughing wakened up the cock which the smith carried dozing in his arms. The cock leapt up on his left shoulder, flapped his wings, then crowed loud and long. The sound of the cock crowing seemed to enrage the fairies; and, in spite of the Bible, they seized the smith and his son and threw them out of the cavern along with the cock. The dirk from the threshold was pulled out and thrown after them and in a minute all was dark and quiet with no sign of the entrance.

The smith went home with his son but for over a year the boy never did any work and hardly spoke a word to any person. One day, the boy who was growing into a fine young man was sitting in the smithy watching his father finishing a very special sword he was making for the local clan chief. The smith was being very careful in his work when suddenly the boy said to his father: 'That is not the way to do it,' and taking the tools from his father's hands he set to work to finish the sword while his father looked on with pleasure. The boy soon made a sword the like of which had never been seen before.

From that day on the youth worked constantly with his father and became the inventor of fine and well-made weapons, the making of which kept them both in steady employment. Their fame for sword-making spread throughout the land and they were both very happy. It was said that the secret of good sword-making must have been discovered by the son while living with the fairies.

The fox and the wolf

The last wolf living wild in Scotland was killed by hunters in Sutherlandshire many years ago but before this happened it came about that a fox and a wolf shared a cave near the sea shore on the Mull of Kintyre at a place known as the 'Land's End' of Scotland. Now, the fox is well known for being very clever and, as a result, was looked upon with suspicion by other animals, especially the wolf.

Before he took up his abode with the fox this wolf was standing taking a drink at the edge of a river which ran into the sea. On looking up after drinking the cool, clear water he saw the fox hunting about among the whin bushes on the other side of the river. As he watched he saw the fox pick up in his mouth a large piece of wool from one of the bushes where the sheep had been rubbing to cast off their old wool. The fox went to the edge of the river and put his bushy tail into the water. Then he went slowly backwards into the river and started to swim to the other side with only his nose and the piece of wool showing above the surface. Before reaching the bank where the wolf was standing he put his head and nose under the water and allowed the piece of wool to float away.

As the fox left the river the wolf spoke to him, saying: 'Why do you wash your tail first, surely the best way is to wash your face first?'

The fox replied: 'I do not scratch like a silly wolf to rid myself of stupid little fleas who run from my tail and body when they are covered by water and all land in the wool carried in my mouth which I then allow to float away.'

'How clever,' remarked the wolf. Being a close relative and thinking that he might learn some tricks, the wolf suggested that they might live and hunt together over the winter months when food was scarce. The fox agreed and they both went to live in the same cave.

One dark night there was a great storm and a ship on its return journey from Ireland suffered damage and part of the cargo was washed overboard. On the morning after the storm the fox and the wolf went down to the shore to see if they could find anything to eat. They found the shore strewn with wreckage, including a full keg of Irish butter which they immediately rolled away into their cave.

When the keg was safe in the cave the wolf started to lick his lips and suggested that they might set to work and break it open but the sly fox was also very fond of butter and had decided that he would eat it all himself.

'No, we will not break it open yet but should wait until the snow has covered the ground and food is scarce. We will bury it in soft ground and dig it up when we are very hungry,' said the fox.

The wolf was very disappointed, but he thought that saving the butter for hard times was a very clever idea. He did not suspect that the fox would cheat him and they both set about to bury the keg in soft ground some distance from the cave.

Some days after the keg had been buried the fox came

back to the cave with a sly look in his eyes. 'Oh dear, oh dear,' he sighed, 'life is a heavy burden.'

'What has happened?' asked the wolf who was very soft-hearted. The fox then explained that he had been asked to visit a friend who dwelt over the high hills and that the journey would make him very tired.

'Do you need to go? Make some excuse when next you see your friend,' said the wolf.

'That I cannot do,' answered the fox, 'for my friend has asked me to be godfather at a christening.'

That evening, the fox was absent and the wolf was left alone in the cave. The sly fox did not go to any christening but went to where the keg of butter was buried. He uncovered the keg and had a good meal of Irish butter. He replaced the covering on the keg before leaving the hiding place, then went hunting about the local farmyards. At midnight he came back to the cave and claimed that he had had a good meal at the christening and was very tired. Every week afterwards the fox always made excuses to leave the cave alone at night and continued to tell lies to the wolf who was becoming very suspicious. The fox was becoming fat and sleek while the poor wolf was thin and hungry as the food which they shared in the cave was becoming scarce.

One night, the wolf was very hungry and after the fox had left with the usual excuse of visiting friends he went hunting in the high hills where he chanced to meet another friendly wolf who was also out hunting. The wolf from the cave told him about living with the fox.

'Has he a very bushy tail, always tells lies, and washes himself by going into a river tail first?' asked the new friend.

'Yes, I think it is the same,' was the reply.

'Then look at my tail which is only a stump and listen to that which I have to tell you about that sly animal,' continued the friendly voice.

He was then told what happened during a very cold, frosty night the previous winter when the friendly wolf and the sly fox were searching for food in a farmyard beside a duck pond. The fox said that he could smell a nice cheese, pointing to the edge of the duck pond where a round, yellow image was to be seen.

'How can we get it out if it is a cheese?' said the wolf.

'Well,' replied the fox, 'you stop here till I see if the farmer is asleep and I will fetch a pole. You lie down at the edge and keep your tail on it, nobody will see you or know that it is there but keep your tail steady as I may be some time coming back.' The sly fox was well aware that the round, yellow image was not a cheese but the reflection of the moon on the surface of the pond which was starting to freeze up. He also wanted to be rid of the wolf so that he would have more food for himself. So, after waiting for some time to make sure that the tail of the wolf had frozen to the surface of the pond he awakened the farmer and his wife by disturbing all the animals about the farm.

The farmer and his wife came out with sticks and immediately saw the wolf. 'I thought they were going to kill me but when I tried to run away my tail was frozen in the pond. I managed to escape but lost most of my tail and that is why I have only a stump. Beware of the sly fox,' said the friendly wolf.

The wolf returned to the cave and thought about what

he had been told by his friend. In the morning the larder was bare and snow covered the ground.

'Let us go and dig up the keg of butter,' said the wolf. The fox agreed and the two set out for the place where the keg was hidden. They scraped away the earth and uncovered the keg only to find that it was empty.

'This is your work,' said the fox, turning to the poor innocent wolf. 'Not I,' replied the wolf. 'I have never been near the spot since we buried it together.'

Back they both went to the cave, arguing all the way, the fox declaring that the wolf must have taken the butter, and the wolf protesting his innocence and still thinking about the strange story he had been told by the wolf from the hills. 'Are you prepared to swear to your innocence?' said the fox at last. 'Yes, I am,' replied the wolf, and standing in the middle of the cave holding up one paw he solemnly swore:

> *'If it be that I stole the butter:*
> *May a fateful disease fall on me.'*

When he finished he put down his paw and turning to the fox said, 'It is your turn now. I have sworn and you must do the same.'

The fox was worried for although he was both untruthful and dishonest now, he had been well brought up in his youth and was afraid of swearing falsely. He had no courage to tell the truth and at last he was forced to swear an oath also. He swore:

> *'If it be me that stole the butter:*
> *Then let some deadly punishment fall on me.'*

After he had heard him swear this terrible oath, the wolf

thought that his suspicions might be groundless, but he was still not certain.

The wolf then thought of a sure test to find out if the fox had sworn a false oath. He suggested that they both go into the local smithy while the blacksmith was away having his dinner and sit in front of the forge fire to keep themselves warm. The wolf was now becoming just as clever as the fox. He knew that by sitting in front of the forge fire whoever had eaten the butter would ooze out fat.

The fox was forced to agree to the fire test and they both went into the smithy. After a few minutes of sitting in front of the forge fire the wolf saw that the fox was beginning to have a greasy look on his fur. Just then the sound of a horse approaching the smithy was heard and they were forced to leave. They waited outside and saw the horse being taken into the smithy by a farm boy who left the horse near the door and went away in search of the blacksmith.

'Now is my chance to pay back this sly fox,' thought the wolf, and he said to his companion: 'There is a notice on the smithy door which I cannot read because my eyesight is failing. Try and read it for me. It could be for a sale of poultry where we might find food.' The fox, in addition to being sly, was very vain and he did not like to confess that from where they were standing his eyes were no better than the wolf's. He edged closer to the door, near where the horse was standing. The wolf then gave a loud howl which caused the horse to take fright. The horse kicked out with its hind legs, struck the fox, and killed him stone dead.

The old saying had come true. *'Be sure your sin will find you out.'*

The elfin knight

There is a lone moor in Scotland which in bygone times was said to be haunted by an elfin knight. The knight was only seen at rare intervals, about once in seven years, and always when the moon was full, but the people of the country round about the moor had a genuine fear. This fear was caused by people disappearing on their way across the moor. They were never heard of again. When people went missing on the moor the men of the local villages banded together and made a search but they were always unsuccessful. The search party would then whisper to one another that the missing person had fallen into the hands of the dreaded knight.

As a result, the moor was deserted as nobody dared pass that way or even live close by. It then became the haunt of all sorts of wild animals who found that they were never disturbed by mortal huntsmen.

Some distance from the moor lived two young earls, Earl St Clair and Earl Gregory, who were very good friends. They rode and hunted together and in time of war fought together against the enemy. They were both fearless and fond of hunting. It was Earl Gregory who suggested that one day they should go hunting on the moor in spite of the elfin knight. 'I do not believe in the story of the elfin knight. It is just an old wives' tale made up to frighten the bairns,' said Earl Gregory. 'It is also a pity that so much good hunting is lost because of the story of the elfin knight.'

Earl St Clair did not agree with him: 'It is meddling with the unknown,' he answered, 'and it is no bairn's tale that travellers have set out to cross the moor and never be seen again.' But he agreed that it was a pity that so much good sport was lost. He also said that they might be safe from any power that the elfin knight may have if they were to wear the sign of the Blessed Trinity bound to their arms for all to see.

Earl Gregory burst out laughing at this suggestion. 'Do you think I am one of the bairns?' he said. 'First to be frightened by an idle tale and then to think that a leaf of clover will protect me? No, no, carry the sign if you wish, but I will trust in my good bow and arrow.'

Earl St Clair did not heed his companion's words, for he remembered that his mother had told him when he was a little boy at her knee that whoever carried the sign of the Blessed Trinity need never fear any spell made by warlock, witch, elf or demon. So he went out to the meadow and plucked a leaf of clover which he bound on his arm with a silken scarf; then he mounted his horse and rode with Earl Gregory to the desolate and lonely moorland.

For some hours all went well and in the heat of the chase the young earls forgot their fears. Then suddenly they both reined in their horses and sat gazing in front of them with fear marked on their faces. A horseman had crossed their track, but who he was and where he came from was a mystery.

'He rides in haste, whoever he may be,' said Earl Gregory, 'and I thought that no horse on earth could match mine for swiftness. Let us follow him and see where he is going.'

'The Lord forbid that you follow him for it is the elfin knight,' said Earl St Clair. 'Can you not see that he is not riding on the solid ground but flies through the air; although the horse seems to be mortal it has wings on its feet like those of a bird to carry it through the air. It will be an evil day for you if you try to follow.'

Earl St Clair forgot that he carried a talisman which his companion lacked and he was able to see things which the other's eyes could not see. He was startled and amazed when Earl Gregory said sharply, 'I see no wings, your mind has gone mad over this elfin knight. I tell you that he who passed was a good knight, clad in green and riding a great German horse. I love a gallant horseman and I will follow him to find out who he is if it means going to the world's end.'

Without another word he put spurs to his horse and galloped off in the direction which the mysterious stranger had taken, leaving Earl St Clair alone upon the moorland, his fingers touching the sacred sign and his lips muttering prayers for protection for he knew that his friend had been bewitched. He then made up his mind that he would also follow and try to remove the spell which had been cast over his friend.

Meanwhile Earl Gregory rode on and on, ever following in the wake of the knight in green, over moor, burn and moss, until he came to the most desolate region that he had ever seen in his life. The wind blew cold as if from snowfields and the white hoar frost lay thick on the withered grass at his feet, but in front of him was a sight from which mortal men might well shrink back in awe and dread. He saw an enormous ring marked on the ground, inside which the grass, instead of being withered and frozen, was lush and green. Hundreds of shadowy elfin figures were dancing, clad in loose transparent robes of dull blue, which seemed to curl and twist round the wearers like wreaths of smoke.

These weird goblins were shouting and singing as they danced and waving their arms above their heads. Some were throwing themselves about on the ground as if they had gone mad. Earl Gregory halted his horse outside the ring and when he was seen by the dancers they stopped and beckoned to him with their skinny fingers. 'Come hither, come hither,' they shouted: 'Come tread a measure with us and afterwards we will drink to thee out of our monarch's loving cup.'

Strange as it may seem, the spell that had been cast over the young earl was so powerful that, in spite of his fear on observing the dancers, he felt that he must obey the summons to enter into the ring. He threw his bridle on his horse's neck and prepared to join them, but just then an old and grizzled goblin stepped out from among his companions and approached the edge of the ring. It appeared that he could not leave the charmed circle for he stopped at the edge of it, then stooping down he pretended to pick up something from the ground and whispered to the young earl: 'I know not who you are or from whence you come, Sir Knight, but if you love your life do not come within this ring or join with us in our feast or you will live to regret it.'

Earl Gregory only laughed at the warning. 'I vowed

that I would follow the Green Knight,' he replied, 'and this I will do to carry out my vow, even if it takes me to the end of the world.' With these words he stepped over the edge of the circle right in amongst the ghostly dancers.

At his coming they shouted louder than ever and danced more madly, until all at once they became silent. They parted to form two companies, leaving a clear way through their ranks where they indicated that the young earl should walk. On walking through the ranks he came to the middle of the circle and there, seated at a table of red marble, was the knight whom he had come so far to seek. He was still clad in his grass-green robes and before him on the table stood a wondrous goblet fashioned from gold with emeralds set round the rim and blood-red rubies clustered round the base. This goblet was filled with heather ale which foamed over the rim. When the knight saw Earl Gregory he lifted the goblet from the table and handed it to him with a stately bow. The young earl was very thirsty and he was glad of the drink. As he drank he noticed that the ale in the goblet never grew less, but was always foaming up to the edge of the rim. For the first time his heart misgave him and he wished that he had never set out on this strange adventure.

But, alas, the time for regrets had passed, for already a strange numbness was coming over his limbs and a chill pallor was creeping over his face. Before he could utter a single cry for help the goblet dropped from his nerveless fingers. He then fell down before the elfin king like a dead man. A great shout of triumph went up from all the gathered company for it filled their hearts with joy to think that they had enticed some unwary mortal to their ring and were able to throw their uncanny spell over him so that he must spend long years in their company.

As soon as their shouts of triumph began to fade away they started muttering and whispering to each other with looks of fear on their faces. Their keen ears had heard a sound of human footsteps which were so free that they knew at once that the stranger approaching, whoever he was, had not been touched by any spell or charm. If this were so he might work ill against them and rescue their captive from the ring.

What they dreaded was true; for it was the brave Earl St Clair who approached, fearless and strong because of the holy sign which he wore. As soon as he saw the ring and the company of dancers he was about to step over its magic border when the little grizzled goblin who had whispered to Earl Gregory came and whispered to him also. 'Alas, alas,' he exclaimed with a look of sorrow on his wrinkled face. 'Have you come, as your companion came, to pay toll of years to the elfin king? If you have, turn back before it is too late.'

'Who are you and where do you come from?' asked the earl, looking kindly down at the little creature in front of him. 'I came from your country,' wailed the goblin. 'I was once a mortal man, even as you, but I set out over the enchanted moor and the elfin king appeared in the guise of a noble knight. I followed him and drank the ale from the goblet. I am now doomed to stay here for seven long years.' The little old goblin explained that Earl Gregory had also taken the accursed drink of ale and was now lying as if dead at the monarch's feet, but he would awaken in the form of an old grizzled goblin and be kept in bondage.

'What can I do to rescue him before he takes on the elfin shape?' cried Earl St Clair. 'I have no fear of the spell of this cruel captor for I wear the sign of one who is stronger. Speak, little man, for time is pressing.'

'There *is* something you can do, Sir Earl, but if you fail no power can save you or your companion.'

'What is it?' asked the earl impatiently.

'You must remain motionless,' answered the little old man, 'in the cold and frost until dawn is breaking and the hour comes when they sing matins in the holy church. You must then walk slowly nine times round the edge of the enchanted ring, then afterwards walk boldly across to the red marble table where sits the elfin king. On the table you will see the golden goblet filled with heather ale. You must then pick up the goblet and carry it away without saying a word. This enchanted ground on which we dance may look solid to mortal eyes but it is a quaking bog with a dark loch underneath wherein dwells a fearsome monster. If you so much as utter one word while your feet are on the bog you will fall through and be killed by the monster.' So saying, the goblin stepped back among his companions of the dance, leaving Earl St Clair standing alone at the edge of the ring.

He waited shivering with cold through the long, dark hours of the night until the grey dawn was breaking over the far mountaintops. With the coming of the dawn the elfin forms seemed to dwindle and fade away. At the hour when the sound of the matin bell came softly pealing from across the moor, he began his solemn walk round and round the ring. He heard murmurs of anger like distant thunder from the elfin shadows and the very ground seemed to heave and quiver as if to shake the bold intruder from its surface. The blessed sign on his arm served him well and Earl St Clair went on unhurt.

When he had finished the required pacing, he stepped boldly on to the enchanted ground and walked across it. To his astonishment he found all the ghostly elves and goblins whom he had seen were lying frozen into tiny blocks of ice. It was hard for him to walk without treading on them. As he approached the marble table the very hairs rose on his head at the sight of the elfin king sitting behind it, stiff and stark like his followers. In front of him lay the form of Earl Gregory who had shared the same fate but was still in mortal form.

Nothing stirred except two black ravens who sat, one on each side of the marble table, as if to guard the golden goblet, flapping their wings and croaking hoarsely.

When Earl St Clair lifted the precious cup the ravens rose in the air and circled round his head screaming with rage. The frozen elves and their mighty king were also stirring from their frozen sleep. The king half sat up as if to lay hands on the intruder but the power of the holy sign restrained them all. As he retraced his steps, awesome and terrible were the sounds he heard around him. The ravens continued to shriek and the half-frozen goblins screamed. From the hidden loch below, the deep breathing of the monster could be heard where it was lurking there eager for prey.

The brave earl paid no attention but kept steadily onwards carrying the golden goblet. Just as the sound of

the matin bell was dying away in the morning air he stepped on to solid ground once more and immediately flung the enchanted goblet away from the edge of the ring. At once every elf vanished along with their king and his marble table. Nothing was left on the green grass save Earl Gregory who was slowly awakening from his frozen slumber. He stretched himself and stood up shaking in every limb. He gazed around as if wondering where he was.

Earl St Clair ran to him and took him in his arms until the senses returned and the warm blood coursed through his veins. The two friends returned to the spot where Earl St Clair had thrown down the goblet only to find pieces of rough grey whinstone.

For ever after, thanks to the brave earl, the moor was safe for travellers.

The brownie and the green slippers

Brownies were friendly little people usually dressed in green who lived within green hillocks or mounds which are still to be found throughout Scotland. If properly treated, the brownies would carry out housework while the occupants of the house were asleep. It was customary to set down a bowl of cream in the kitchen for the brownie before going to bed. To forget to do this was thought to bring bad luck. Many devices were employed to prevent the household dogs or cats from stealing the cream which was usually set down on the floor. One device was a chalked ring of wavy design surrounding the bowl.

In about 1840, such a brownie lived in the Doune hill at Rothiemurchus across the river Spey from the village of Aviemore. According to legend, this brownie, in return for 'the cream-bowl duly set', worked cleaning pots and pans in the kitchen of the local laird while the household was asleep. One night, the brownie by accident toppled over a stack of pans and the noise awakened the laird who was so upset about his sleep being disturbed that he chased the brownie away. The brownie ran away in fright and in doing so one of his green-coloured shoes was lost in the darkness of the forest. He was afraid to return to the fairy hill as the fairy queen would scold him for the loss of the shoe which was made of very fine skin.

It so happened that the Aviemore shoemaker was on his

way early the next morning to the house of the laird to make dance slippers for his daughters. On his way to the house the shoemaker heard squirrels in the tall Caledonian fir trees which lined both sides of the road, and on looking up saw the brownie sitting on one of the lower branches of a tree. He was crying and told the shoemaker how he had lost his shoe and was unable to return to the fairy hill. He was also sorry about having to leave the house as the daughters of the laird had been very kind to him by leaving out small jars of honey beside the cream-bowl.

The shoemaker, who was carrying his materials and tools, told the brownie that he would sit down at the bottom of the tree and make him a pair of new shoes from fine goatskin. The shoemaker had a small last which he used for making shoes and slippers for the youngest daughter of the laird. From this small last a pair of shoes was made for the brownie but, alas, they were not the colour of fairy green. The brownie then told the shoemaker to gather certain berries and mix them with water from a nearby spring. The result was a brilliant dye of fairy green which the shoemaker used on the shoes he had made for the brownie, who was very pleased. Before leaving to return to the fairy hill the brownie made the shoemaker promise that he would not reveal the secret of the dye which he was only to use on dance slippers for the daughters of the laird.

The brownie never returned to the house of the laird, but 'the cream-bowl duly set' was always left at night in the shoemaker's work shed which was then found clean and tidy in the morning when the shoemaker sat down at his stool. The daughters of the laird often wondered where the shoemaker had obtained the bright everlasting green dye used for their dance slippers. The slippers were much admired whenever they were worn, but the shoemaker never told the secret of the dye.

Thomas the Rhymer

Of all the young gallants in Scotland in the thirteenth century, there was none more gracious and debonair than Thomas Learmont, laird of the Castle of Erceldoune in Berwickshire.

He loved books, poetry and music which were uncommon tastes in those days, and above all he loved to study nature and to watch the habits of the beasts and birds that made their abode in the fields and woods round about his home.

Now it chanced that, one sunny May morning, Thomas left his tower of Erceldoune and went wandering into the woods that lay about the Huntly Burn, a little stream that came rushing down from the slopes of the Eildon Hills. It was a lovely morning, fresh and bright with a gentle, warm breeze. The tender leaves were bursting out of their sheaths and covering all the trees with a fresh soft mantle of green. At his feet the yellow primroses and starry anemones were turning up their faces to the morning sky. The birds were singing and hundreds of insects were flying backwards and forwards in the sunshine.

Thomas felt so happy with the gladness of it all that he threw himself down at the root of a tree. As he was lying there he heard the trampling of horse's hooves as the animal forced its way through the bushes. On looking up he saw a most beautiful lady riding towards him on a grey horse. The lady wore a hunting dress of glistening silk the colour of fresh spring grass. From her shoulders hung a velvet mantle of the same colour. Her hair was like rippling gold and hung loosely round her shoulders. On her head sparkled a diadem of precious stones which flashed like fire in the morning sunlight.

Her saddle was made of pure ivory and the saddle cloth of blood-red satin. The saddle girths were of corded silk and her stirrups of cut crystal. The reins were of beaten gold all hung with silver bells, so that, as she rode along, the bells made a sound like fairy music.

The lady carried a hunting horn and a sheaf of arrows. She was accompanied by hunting dogs which ran loose at her horse's side. As she rode down the glen she lilted part of an old song. Thomas knelt by the side of the path to pay homage as he thought she must be the queen. When the rider came forward she shook her head sadly and said: 'I am not the queen of your land. Men call me queen but it is of a faraway country; for I am the Queen of Fairyland.'

It was as if a spell were cast over Thomas, making him forget prudence and caution. He knew that it was dangerous for mortals to meddle with fairies but he was so entranced with the beauty of the lady that he begged her to give him a kiss. This was just what she wanted for if she once kissed him she had him in her power. As soon as their lips met a great change came over her. The mantle and riding skirt of silk seemed to fade away leaving her clad in a long grey garment which was the colour of ashes. Her beauty seemed to fade away and in a second she had become old and wan. On seeing the astonishment and

terror of Thomas she burst into a mocking laugh.

'I am not so fair to look on now,' she said, 'but that matters little for you have sold yourself to be my servant for seven long years.' When he heard these words poor Thomas fell on his knees and begged for mercy. The elfin queen only laughed in his face and brought her grey horse up to where he was standing. 'No, no,' she said, 'you asked for the kiss and must pay the price.' Thomas was forced to mount behind her and the grey horse galloped off.

On and on they went, going more swiftly than the wind till they left the land of Scotland behind and came to the edge of a great desert. It was dry, bare and desolate to the edge of the far horizon. At least so it seemed to the weary eyes of Thomas of Erceldoune. He wondered if he and his strange companion had to cross the vast desert and if so whether there was any chance of reaching the other side.

The fairy queen suddenly tightened the rein and the grey horse stopped its wild gallop. 'Now you must descend to earth, Thomas.' It was also explained that he had to sit on the ground and lay his head on her knee. Thomas dismounted and rested his head on the fairy queen's knee while she also sat on the ground. He then looked once more over the desert and everything seemed to have changed. He now saw three different roads leading across the desert.

One of the roads was broad and level. It ran straight on across the sand so that no one who was travelling by it could possibly lose the way. The second road was different from the first. It was narrow and winding with a thorn hedge on one side and a briar hedge on the other. The hedges were high and tangled and any person travelling along it would appear to have some difficulty.

The third road was unlike either. It was a bonnie road winding up a hillside among brackens and heather with golden-yellow whins nearby. It looked to be a road where travelling would be pleasant.

'Now,' said the fairy queen, 'I will tell you where these three roads lead to.' She then explained that the first road was easy and many might choose to travel on it but it came to a bad end and travellers would repent of their choice for ever. The narrow road with the thorns and briars did not look so good and few bothered to ask where it went to. If they asked, more would be likely to use this second road, for it was the path of righteousness and ended in a glorious city called the City of the Great King.

She further explained that the third road winding up the hillside was the road leading to fair Elfland and that was the road they were going to take.

'Mark thee, Thomas,' said the fairy queen, 'if you ever hope to see your Erceldoune again take care when we reach our journey's end and speak not a single word to anyone save me – for the mortal who openeth his lips to speak rashly in Fairyland must stay there for ever.'

Then she told him to mount behind her on the grey horse again and they rode on. They had not ridden far along the road before it led them into a narrow ravine which seemed to go right down under the earth where the air was dank and heavy. There was no light to guide them and they came to a place where the sound of rushing water was heard. The grey horse seemed to plunge into the water which came up to Thomas's feet and then over his knees.

His courage had been slowly ebbing ever since he had been parted from the daylight but now he gave himself up for lost. It seemed certain that he and his strange companion would never arrive safely at their journey's end. Thomas fell forward in a kind of faint and if it had not been for the tight hold he had of the long, ash-grey garment worn by the fairy queen he would have fallen from the horse and been drowned. At last the darkness began to disappear and the light grew stronger until they were back in bright sunshine.

Thomas then took courage and looked up. He found that they were riding through a beautiful orchard where apples, pears and wineberries were growing in great abundance. His tongue was so parched and dry with the fright of the water that he longed for some of the fruit to restore him. He stretched out his hand to pluck some of the fruit but his companion turned in the saddle and forbade him to touch the fruit. 'There is nothing safe for you to eat here,' she said, 'save an apple, which I will give you presently. If you touch anything else you are bound to remain in Fairyland for ever.'

Poor Thomas had to restrain himself as best he could and they rode slowly on until they came to a tiny tree all covered with apples. The fairy queen bent down from the saddle and plucked one of the apples which was bright red in colour and handed it to her companion. 'This I give to you,' she said, 'and I do it gladly for these apples are the Apples of Truth; and whoever eats them will gain a reward in that his lips will never more be able to frame a lie.' Thomas took the apple and ate it and for evermore the Grace of Truth rested on his lips. That is why in after years men called him 'True Thomas'.

They continued for a little way until they came within sight of a magnificent castle standing on a hillside. 'That is my abode,' said the fairy queen pointing to it proudly. 'There dwells my lord and all his nobles of the court. My lord has a bad temper and will not show any liking for a strange gallant he sees in my company, so beware, do not utter a word to anyone and I will tell them all that you are dumb.'

With these words the lady raised her hunting horn and blew a loud and piercing blast. As she did so a marvellous change came over her again. The ugly, ash-coloured garment dropped off, her grey hair vanished and she appeared once more in her splendid hunting dress and mantle, with long, golden hair and a beautiful complexion. Thomas also noticed that the hunting dogs had reappeared and he found that his own country clothes had been transformed into a suit of fine brown cloth and on his feet he wore a pair of fine satin shoes.

Immediately the sound of the horn rang out the doors of the castle flew open and the king hurried out to meet his queen, accompanied by such a number of knights and ladies, minstrels and page boys that Thomas, who had already slid from his seat on the grey horse, had no difficulty in passing through the castle gates unobserved.

Everyone seemed to be glad that the queen was back again and they all crowded into the great hall where she spoke to them all graciously and allowed them to kiss her hand. She and her husband then went to a dais at the far end of the huge apartment where two thrones stood. The royal pair then seated themselves to watch the revels which now began.

Meanwhile, Thomas stood far away at the other end of

the hall feeling very lonely yet fascinated by the scene on which he was gazing. Although all the fine ladies and courtiers along with the knights were dancing in one part of the hall there were huntsmen coming and going in another part carrying in deer which they had apparently killed while hunting. Rows of cooks were standing beside the deer carcases cutting up the joints and carrying them away to be cooked.

The feasting and dancing went on for three days while Thomas watched, keeping in the background. At the end of the third day the queen rose from her dais and crossed the hall to where Thomas was standing. 'Time to mount and ride, Thomas,' she said, 'if you would like to see the fair Castle of Erceldoune again.' Thomas looked at her in amazement. 'You spoke of seven long years and I have only been here three days.' The queen then explained that time went by quickly in Fairyland. What he thought was three days was in fact seven years. 'I would like you to stay,' said the queen, 'but you might be found out and every seventh year an evil spirit comes and carries away one of our followers and I fear that the evil spirit might choose you.'

The grey horse was brought and Thomas mounted it along with the queen. In a short time they returned to the spot near the tree beside the Huntly Burn. Before the queen said farewell Thomas asked her to give him something as a parting gift so that he could let people know that he had really been to Fairyland. 'I have already given you the Gift of Truth,' she replied. 'I will now give you the Gifts of Prophecy and Poetry so that you will be able to foretell the future and also write wondrous verses.

Beside the unseen gifts, here is something that mortals can see with their own eyes – a harp that was made in Fairyland. Farewell, my friend, some day perhaps I will return for you again.'

With these words the lady vanished and Thomas was left alone feeling sorry that they had parted. After this he lived for many a long year in his Castle of Erceldoune and the fame of his poetry and of his prophecies spread all over the country so that people named him True Thomas and Thomas the Rhymer. The prophecies were many and it is impossible to write them all down but the following two are well known in the history of Scotland. He foretold the battle of Bannockburn in these words:

> '*The burn of Breid*
> *shall rin fou reid*'

which came to pass on that terrible day when the waters of the little Bannock burn near Stirling were reddened by the blood of the defeated English.

Fourteen long years went by and the people were beginning to forget that Thomas the Rhymer had ever been in Fairyland. At last a day came when Scotland was at war with England and the Scottish army was resting not far from the Castle of Erceldoune. Thomas determined to make a feast and invited all the nobles and barons who were leading the army to sup with him. The feast was long remembered, everything was as magnificent as was possible, and when the meal was ended Thomas rose in his place and taking his elfin harp he sang to his assembled guests song after song of the days of long ago.

The guests had never heard such wonderful music and

that very night after all the guests had gone back to their tents a soldier on guard saw in the moonlight a snow-white hart and hind moving slowly down the road that ran past the camp. There was something so unusual about the animals that the soldier called to his officer to come and look at them. The officer called to his brother officers and soon there was quite a crowd softly following the dumb creatures who paced solemnly on as if they were keeping time to music unheard by mortal ears.

'There is something uncanny about this,' said one soldier. 'Let us send for Thomas of Erceldoune who may be able to tell us if it be an omen or not.' 'Aye, send for Thomas of Erceldoune,' cried everyone at once. A little page boy was then sent to rouse the Rhymer from his slumbers. When he heard the boy's message, the seer's face grew grave and rapt.

'Tis a summons,' he said softly, 'a summons from the Queen of Fairyland. I have waited long for it and it has come at last.' Thomas then went outside and instead of joining the company of waiting men he walked straight up to the snow-white hart and hind. As soon as he reached them they paused for a moment as if to greet him. Then all three moved slowly down a steep bank to the Huntly Burn and disappeared in its foaming waters as the burn was in full flood at the time.

Although a careful search was made no trace of Thomas of Erceldoune was ever found. It is said to this day that the hart and hind were messengers from the elfin queen and that Thomas went back to Fairyland with them.

The Dwarfie Stone

Far up in a green valley on the island of Hoy stands an immense boulder. The boulder is hollow inside and the people of the Orkney Islands call it the Dwarfie Stone, because long centuries ago, so the legend has it, Snorro the dwarf lived there.

Nobody knew where Snorro came from or how long he had lived in the dark chamber inside the Dwarfie Stone. All that they knew about him was that he was a little man with a queer, twisted, deformed body and a face of marvellous beauty which never seemed to look any older but was always smiling and young.

Men said that this was because Snorro's father had been a fairy who had bequeathed to his son the gift of everlasting youth to compensate for the twisted deformed body. But no one knew for certain.

One thing was certain, however. He had inherited from his mother, who had been mortal, the dangerous qualities of vanity and ambition. The longer he lived the more vain and ambitious he became. He always carried a mirror of polished steel on a chain round his neck so that he could look into it and see the reflection of his handsome face. The people of the island went to him for help when they were ill as he spent most of his time collecting herbs from the hillside and in his dark abode he made medicines and potions from them. He always charged high prices for the assistance given.

Not very far from the Dwarfie Stone there was a curious hill shaped exactly like a wart. It was known as the Wart Hill of Hoy and men said that somewhere on the side of the hill was hidden a wonderful coloured stone and whoever found it would have health, wealth and happiness for ever. Everything, in fact, that a human person would desire.

They believed that this magic stone could be seen on the hillside at certain times if the people looking for it were at the right spot at the right moment.

Now Snorro had made up his mind that he would find the magic stone. During his wanderings to find herbs he kept a lookout for the stone and at night when everyone was asleep he would creep out with pick and spade to turn over the ground in the hope of finding it.

He was always accompanied in his searching by a large grey-headed raven who lived with him in the Dwarfie Stone cave. The islanders feared this bird of ill omen as much, perhaps, as they feared its master; for, although they went to consult Snorro in all their difficulties, bought medicine and love potions from him, they looked upon him with a certain dread. They felt that there was something weird and uncanny about him.

At the time of Snorro the Orkney Islands were governed by two earls who were half-brothers. Paul, the elder, was a tall, handsome man with dark hair and brown eyes. All the country people loved him, for he was so skilled and had such a loving nature that no one could help being fond of him. This was more remarkable because, with all his winning manner, he had such a lack of conversation that he was called 'Paul the Silent'.

Harold, on the other hand, was as different from his brother as night from day. He was fair-haired and blue-eyed. He also gained for himself the name of 'Harold the Orator', because he was always free of speech and ready with his tongue. Harold was not a favourite with the people. He was haughty, jealous and quick-tempered. He was well aware that the people liked his silent brother best and this knowledge made him envious with the result that a coldness sprang up between them.

It happened one summer that Earl Harold went on a visit to the King of Scotland accompanied by his mother, the Countess Helga, and her sister, the Countess Fraukirk. While at the court in Scotland, Harold met a charming young Irish lady, the Lady Morna, who had come from Ireland to attend the Scottish queen. She was so sweet and good and gentle that Earl Harold's heart was won. He made up his mind that she should be his bride. Although he paid her great attention the Lady Morna had seen glimpses of his jealous temper and she had no wish to marry him. When she refused the offer of marriage Earl Harold ground his teeth in silent rage. He saw it was no use pressing his suit at the Scottish court but was determined to obtain the consent by guile.

Accordingly, he begged his mother to persuade the Lady Morna to go back with them on a visit hoping that when she was alone with him in Orkney he would be able to overcome her prejudice against him.

The Lady Morna, thinking no evil, accepted the Countess Helga's invitation and no sooner had the party arrived back in Orkney than Paul, charmed with the grace and beauty of the fair Irish maiden, fell head over heels in love with her. And the Lady Morna, from the very first hour that she saw him, returned his love.

This state of affairs could not remain hidden and when Harold realized what had happened his anger and jealousy knew no bounds. Seizing a dagger, he rushed up to the turret where his brother was sitting and threatened to stab him to the heart if he did not promise to give up all thought of winning the lovely stranger.

Paul was not afraid. 'Calm thyself, brother,' he said. 'It is true that I love the lady, but that is no proof that I shall win her. Is it likely that she will choose me whom all men call "Paul the Silent" when she has a chance of marrying you whose tongue moves so swiftly and you have the proud title of Harold the Orator?'

At these words Harold's vanity was flattered and he thought that after all his step-brother was right and that he had very little chance with his meagre gift of speech. Harold then threw down the dagger and shaking hands with Paul begged his pardon for the unkind thoughts.

By this time it was coming near to the Feast of Yule when it was the custom for the earl and his court to leave Kirkwall and stay for some weeks at the Palace of Orphir some nine miles distant. In order to see that everything was ready at the palace, Earl Paul left some days before the others. The evening before Paul left he chanced to find the Lady Morna sitting alone in one of the deep windows of the great hall. She had been weeping, and was full of sadness at the thought of Paul's departure. At the sight of her distress the young earl could no longer contain himself. He folded her in his arms and whispered how much he loved her and begged her to promise to be his wife. She agreed willingly and confessed that she had loved him from the very first day she had seen him.

For a little time they sat together rejoicing in their new-found happiness. Then Earl Paul sprang to his feet. 'Let us go and tell the good news to my mother and my brother,' he said. 'Harold may be disappointed at first for he would fain have thee for his own. But his good heart will soon overcome all that and he will rejoice with us also.'

The Lady Morna shook her head. She knew better than her lover what Earl Harold's feelings would be. 'Let us hold our peace till after Yule,' she pleaded. 'It will be a joy to keep our secret to ourselves for a little while. There will be time enough then to let all the world know.'

Reluctantly, Earl Paul agreed and next day he set off for the Palace of Orphir, leaving his lady love behind.

Little did he guess the danger he was in, for unknown to him his step-aunt, Countess Fraukirk, had been in hiding behind a curtain in the great hall and had overheard every word spoken by the young lovers. Her heart was filled with rage as she had always hated Earl Paul who was not a blood relation and stood in the way of his brother, her own nephew, for, if Paul were dead Harold would be the sole Earl of Orkney. She believed that he had stolen the heart of the Lady Morna whom her own nephew loved. Her hate and anger knew no bounds and she hastened off to her sister's chamber as soon as the lovers had parted. There the two women remained talking together until the chilly dawn broke in the sky.

Next day a boat was seen speeding over the narrow channel to the island of Hoy and in it sat a woman. Her face was hidden behind a dark veil and she was covered from head to foot by a black cloak. Snorro the dwarf knew her even before she took off the cloak and veil, for Countess Fraukirk was no stranger to him. In the course of her long life she had often crossed to Hoy seeking the aid of Snorro to help her in her evil deeds. She always paid him well for any service and he therefore welcomed her gladly. When Snorro heard the nature of her errand his smiling face grew grave and he shook his head. 'I have served you well in the past, Lady,' he said, 'but I think that this thing you ask is beyond my courage. To compass an earl's death is a weighty matter, especially when he is so well loved as is Earl Paul. I have taken my abode in this lonely spot but I hope one day to find the magic stone and if I am suspected of causing the death of Earl Paul I would have to flee for my life without finding the stone. No, I cannot do it.'

The wily countess offered him much gold and lastly she promised to obtain for him a high post at the court of the King of Scotland, and having such wealth and success he would not need to look for the magic stone. At last he consented to do what she asked. 'I will summon my magic loom,' he said, 'and weave a piece of cloth of the finest texture and marvellous beauty, but before I weave it I will poison the thread with a magic potion so that when the cloth is made into a garment, whoever puts it on will die within a few minutes.'

'You are a clever knave,' answered the countess with a cruel smile on her face, 'and you shall be rewarded. Let me have two yards of this wonderful web and I will make a bonnie waistcoat for my fine young earl and give it to him as a yuletide gift. Then I reckon he will not see the year out.' The two parted after arranging that the cloth be delivered to the Palace of Orphir on the day before Christmas Eve.

While Countess Fraukirk had been away upon her wicked errand strange happenings were taking place at the castle at Kirkwall for Harold, encouraged by his brother's absence, offered his heart and hand once more to the Lady Morna. Once more she refused and to save further trouble told him that she had plighted her troth to Earl Paul.

Harold was mad with anger on receiving this information. He rushed out of the palace, flung himself upon his horse, and rode away towards the seashore. While he was galloping wildly along his eyes fell on the mist-covered hills of Hoy rising up across the strip of sea dividing the one island from the other. His thoughts turned to Snorro the dwarf whom he had had occasion to visit as well as his aunt. 'Stupid fool am I,' he said. 'I will go to Snorro and buy from him a love potion which will make my Lady Morna hate my precious brother and turn her thoughts to me.'

He managed to hire a boat and soon he was speeding over the tossing waters on his way to Hoy. On arrival, he hurried up the lonely valley to where the Dwarfie Stone stood. He had no difficulty in finding Snorro who was standing at the hole which served as a door and gazing at the setting sun with his raven perched on his shoulder. 'What brings you here, Sir Earl?' he asked gaily as he scented more gold.

'I come for a love potion,' said Harold; and without more ado he told the whole story to the dwarf. Snorro looked at him from head to foot.

'Blind must be the maiden who needeth a love potion to make her fancy so gallant a knight, Sir Orator.'

Earl Harold laughed angrily. 'It is easier to catch a sunbeam than a woman's roving fancy,' he replied. 'I have no time for jesting, time and tide wait for no man so I need not expect the tide to wait for me. The potion I must have instantly.'

Snorro saw that he was in earnest but did not tell him of the arrangement he had made with Countess Fraukirk as he was sure of a good reward of gold for the love potion. So without a word he entered his dwelling and in a few minutes returned with a phial in his hand which was full of a pink-coloured liquid. 'Pour the contents of this into the Lady Morna's wine cup and before twenty-four hours have passed she will love you better than you love her,' instructed Snorro. After handing over the phial in exchange for a bag of gold he waved his hand and disappeared into his dwelling-place.

Earl Harold returned to the castle at Kirkwall with all speed but it was two days before he had a chance to pour the love potion into the Lady Morna's wine cup. At last, one night at supper he found an opportunity of doing so and, waving away a little page boy, he handed the cup to her himself. Lady Morna raised it to her lips but only made a pretence of drinking as she had seen the hated earl doing something to the cup and she feared some form of treachery. When he had gone back to his seat and was looking away she managed to pour the whole of the wine on to the flagstone floor. Harold turned his head and Lady Morna smiled to herself as she saw the look of satisfaction that came over his face as she put down the empty cup.

From that moment she felt so afraid of Harold that she treated him with great kindness, hoping that by doing so she would be able to keep in his good graces until the court moved to Orphir where her own true love could protect her.

Harold was delighted with her graciousness and he felt certain that the love potion was beginning to work. A week later the court moved to the royal palace at Orphir where Earl Paul had everything in readiness for the reception of his guests. He was overjoyed to meet Lady Morna again and in turn she felt that she was now safe from the unwelcome attentions of Earl Harold who could scarcely contain himself from anger when he saw the meeting of the two lovers. However, he still hoped that the love potion would work and held back his anger.

As for Countess Fraukirk and Countess Helga, they looked forward eagerly to the time when the web of magic cloth would arrive. At last, the day before Christmas Eve, the two wicked women were sitting in the Countess Helga's chamber talking of the time when Earl Harold would rule alone in Orkney, when a tap was heard at the window. On looking round they saw Dwarf Snorro's grey-headed raven perched on the sill with a sealed packet in its beak. They opened the casement and with a hoarse croak the bird let the packet drop on to the floor. It then flapped its great wings and rose slowly into the air again and turned in the direction of Hoy.

With fingers trembling with excitement they broke the seals and undid the packet to find a piece of beautiful material finer than silk and woven in all the colours of the rainbow. 'It will make a bonnie waistcoat,' exclaimed Countess Fraukirk with an unholy laugh. 'The silent earl will be a braw man when he gets it on.' They immediately set to work to cut out and sew the garment.

All that night they worked and most of the next day until late in the afternoon when they were putting in the last stitches and decorating it with gold, hurried footsteps were heard ascending the winding staircase and Earl Harold burst into the chamber. His cheeks were red with passion for he could not but notice that since arriving at Orphir and under her lover's protection Lady Morna had grown very cold and distant towards him. He was beginning to lose faith in Snorro's love potion.

Angry and disappointed he had sought his mother's room to pour out his story of vexation to her, but he stopped short when he saw the wonderful waistcoat lying on the table. It was like a fairy garment and its beauty took his breath away. 'For whom is that?' he asked, pointing to the garment.

'It is a Christmas present for your brother Paul,' answered his mother and she would have gone on to tell him the whole plot and how deadly the waistcoat was.

Alas, her words fanned his anger and he snatched the garment from the table. 'Everything is for Paul, but he shall not have this,' cried Harold. His mother and his aunt threw themselves at his feet and begged him to put down the waistcoat warning him of the poisoned threads. He paid no heed and rushed from the room, putting on the garment at the same time. He ran downstairs with a reckless laugh intending to show the Lady Morna how fine he looked. He had scarcely gained the hall when he fell to the ground in great pain.

Everyone in the hall crowded round him and the two countesses, terrified by what had happened, ran downstairs and tried in vain to tear the waistcoat from his body. It was too late as the deadly poison acting with the heat from his body had done its work. Waving them all aside he turned to his brother Paul who in great distress had knelt down and taken him tenderly in his arms.

'I wronged thee, Paul,' he gasped. 'You have been true and kind. Forgive me in my thoughts,' and gathering up his strength for the last time he pointed to the two wretched women who had brought on all this misery. 'Beware of those two women, for they seek to take your life.' Then his head sank back on his brother's shoulder and with one long sigh he died.

When he learned what had happened and understood where the cloth for the waistcoat came from and for what purpose it had been intended the anger of the Silent Earl knew no bounds. He swore a great oath that Harold would be avenged, and that not only Snorro the dwarf but also his wicked stepmother and her cruel sister would be punished.

But his vengeance was forestalled for in the panic and confusion that followed Harold's death the two countesses made their escape and fled to their castle in the north of Scotland. However, retribution fell on them in the end, as it always does sooner or later on everyone who is so wicked, or selfish or cruel. Norsemen invaded their land in the north and set fire to their castle. They both perished in the flames.

When Earl Paul found that they had escaped he set out in haste for the island of Hoy for he was determined that the dwarf should not escape, but on reaching the Dwarfie Stone he found it silent and deserted. All trace of the uncanny occupant and his raven had disappeared. No one knew what had become of them, although most of the islanders believed that the Powers of the Air had spirited them away and shut them up in some unknown place as a punishment for their wickedness. At any rate, Snorro and his raven were never seen again by any living person and he lost all chance of finding the magic stone.

As for the Silent Earl and his Irish sweetheart, they were married as soon as Earl Harold's funeral was over, and for hundreds of years afterwards when the inhabitants of the Orkney Isles wished to express great happiness, they said, 'As happy as Earl Paul and the Countess Morna.'

Habetrot the spinstress

In bygone days, in an old farmhouse which stood by a river, there lived a beautiful girl called Maisie. She stood tall and erect, with auburn hair and blue eyes. She was the prettiest girl in all the valley. One would have thought that she would have been the pride of her mother's heart. Instead, her mother used to sigh and shake her head whenever she looked at her. And why?

Because, in those days, all men were sensible; and instead of looking out for pretty girls to be their wives, they looked out for girls who could cook and spin and who gave promise of becoming notable housewives. Maisie's mother had been an industrious person; but alas, to her great grief and disappointment, her daughter did not take after her.

Maisie loved to be out of doors, chasing butterflies and plucking wild flowers, far better than sitting at her spinning-wheel. So when her mother saw one after another of Maisie's friends, who were not nearly so pretty as she was, getting rich husbands, she sighed and said: 'Woe's me, child, for methinks no brave wooer will ever pause at our door while they see so idle and thoughtless a girl.' But Maisie only laughed.

At last, her mother grew really angry and one bright spring morning she put down three heads of lint on the table, saying sharply, 'I will have no more of this dallying.

People will say that it is my fault that no wooer comes to seek thee. I cannot have thee left on my hands to be laughed at as the idle maid who would not marry. So now you must work and if you have not spun the lint into seven hanks of thread in three days I will speak to the Mother at St Mary's Convent and you will go there and learn to be a nun.'

Now, though Maisie was an idle girl she had no wish to be shut up in a nunnery; so she tried not to think of the sunshine outside, but sat down to work with her distaff.

But, alas! she was so little used to work that she made very slow progress; and although she sat at the spinning-wheel all day and never once went out of doors, she found at night that she had only spun half a hank of yarn. The next day it was even worse for her arms ached so much she could only work very slowly. That night she cried herself to sleep and next morning, seeing that it was impossible to get her task finished, she threw down her distaff in despair and ran out of doors.

Near the house was a deep dell, through which ran a tiny stream. Maisie loved this dell where the flowers grew so abundantly. This morning she ran down to the edge of the stream and seated herself on a large stone.

It was a glorious morning. The hazel trees were newly covered with leaves and the branches nodded over her head. The primroses and sweet-scented violets peeped out from among the grass and a little water wagtail came and perched on a stone in the middle of the stream.

But the poor girl was in no mood that morning to enjoy the flowers and the birds. Instead of watching them as she generally did she hid her face in her hands. She was wondering what would become of her as she did not want to go into the convent where she would be obliged to study very hard to become a good nun.

'And who wants to make a pretty wench like thee into a nun?' asked a queer, cracked voice which seemed to come from close by. Maisie jumped up and stood staring in front of her as if she had been moonstruck. For, just across the stream from where she had been sitting, there was a curious boulder with a round hole in the middle just like a big apple with the core taken out. Maisie knew the stone well as she had often sat upon it and wondered how the funny hole came to be there.

It was no wonder that she stared, for seated on this stone was the queerest little old woman that she had ever seen in her life. Had it not been for her silver hair and the white mutch with the big frill that she wore on her head, Maisie would have taken her for a little girl. She wore a very short skirt which only reached down to her knees.

The face inside the frill of her cap was round and her cheeks were rosy red. She had little black eyes which twinkled merrily as she looked at the startled maiden. On her shoulders was a black and white checked shawl and on her legs, which she dangled over the edge of the boulder, she wore black silk stockings and neat little shoes with large silver buckles. Maisie stood and looked at her for such a long time in silence that the little old woman repeated her question. 'And who wants to make a pretty wench like thee into a nun? More likely that some gallant gentleman should want to make a bride of thee.'

'Oh, no,' answered Maisie, 'my mother says no gentleman would look at me because I cannot spin.'

'Nonsense,' said the little woman. 'Spinning is all very well for old folks like me. Look at my lips, they are long and ugly because they have spun so much, for I always wet my fingers with them to make it easier to draw the thread from the distaff. No, no, take care of your beauty, do not waste it over the spinning-wheel, nor yet in a nunnery.'

'If my mother only thought the same as you,' replied the girl sadly; and encouraged by the old woman's kindly face she told her the whole story.

'Well,' said the old woman, 'I do not like to see pretty girls weep; what if I were able to help and spin the lint for you?'

Maisie thought that the offer was too good to be true, but her new friend bade her run home and fetch the lint. Maisie required no second bidding.

When she returned she handed the bundle to the little lady and was about to ask her where she should meet her in order to get the thread from her when it was spun. A sudden noise behind her made her look round and when she turned again, to her horror and surprise, the old woman had vanished, lint and all.

She rubbed her eyes and looked all round but the old woman was nowhere to be seen. Maisie wondered if she had been dreaming, but no, that could not be, there were her footprints leading up the bank and down again when she had gone home for the lint which had also disappeared. She also saw a wet mark on a stone in the middle of the stream where she stood when she handed the lint to the mysterious little stranger.

What was she to do now? What would her mother say,

when, in addition to not having finished the task that had been given her, she had to confess to having lost the greater part of the lint also? Maisie ran up and down the little dell, hunting amongst the bushes and peeping into every nook and cranny of the bank where the little old woman might have hidden herself. It was all in vain, and at last, tired out with the search, she sat down on the stone once more and presently fell fast asleep.

When she awoke it was evening. The sun had set and the yellow glow on the western horizon was fast giving place to the silvery light of the moon. She was sitting thinking of the curious events of the day and gazing at the great boulder opposite. It seemed to her as if a distant murmur of voices came from it. With one bound she crossed the stream and clambered on to the stone. She was right.

Someone was talking underneath it far down in the ground. She put her ear close to the stone and listened. The voice of the queer little old woman came up through the hole. 'Ho, Ho, my pretty little wench little knows that my name is Habetrot.'

Full of curiosity, Maisie put her eye to the opening and the strangest sight that she had ever seen met her gaze. She seemed to be looking through a telescope into a wonderful little valley. The trees there were brighter and greener than any that she had ever seen before; and there were beautiful flowers, quite different from the flowers that grew in her country. The little valley was carpeted with the most exquisite moss and on this carpet her tiny friend was busily engaged in spinning.

She was not alone, for round her were a circle of other

little old women who were seated on large white stones and they were all spinning away as fast as they could.

Occasionally one would look up and then Maisie saw that they all seemed to have the same long, thick lips that her friend had. She really felt very sorry, as they all looked kind persons and might have been pretty had it not been for this defect.

One of the spinstresses sat by herself and was engaged in winding the thread from the other spinners into hanks. Maisie did not think that this little lady looked so nice as the others. She was dressed entirely in grey and had a big hooked nose. She wore great horn spectacles and seemed to be called Slantlie Mab as Maisie heard Habetrot address her by that name, telling her to make haste and tie up all the thread for it was getting late and time that the young girl had to carry the hanks home to her mother. Maisie did not quite know what to do, or how she was to get the thread, for she did not like to shout down the hole in case the queer old woman should be angry at being watched.

However, Habetrot herself suddenly appeared on the path beside her with the hanks of thread in her hand. 'Oh, thank you, thank you,' cried Maisie. 'What can I do to show you how grateful I am?'

'Nothing,' answered the fairy. 'I do not work for reward. Only do not tell your mother who spun the thread for you.'

It was now late and Maisie lost no time in running home with the precious thread. When she walked into the kitchen she found that her mother had gone to bed. She seemed to have had a busy day, for hanging up in the wide chimney place to dry were seven large black puddings. The fire was low but still bright and clear and the sight of the puddings made Maisie feel that she was hungry and that fried black puddings were very good.

Flinging the thread down on the table, she hastily pulled off her shoes so as not to make a noise and waken her mother. She then took down the frying pan from the shelf, fried one of the black puddings and ate it. She was still feeling hungry so she took another and another until all the black puddings were gone. Then she crept upstairs to her own little bed and fell fast asleep.

Next morning her mother came downstairs before Maisie was awake. She had not been sleeping very soundly for thinking about her daughter's careless ways. Great was her surprise to see on the table the seven beautiful hanks of thread, but on going to the chimney place to take down a black pudding to fry for breakfast she found that all had gone. She did not know whether to laugh for joy that her daughter had been so industrious or to cry for vexation because all the lovely black puddings which she had expected to last the family for a week were gone. In her bewilderment she sang out:

> *'My daughter's spun seven, seven, seven,*
> *My daughter's eaten seven, seven, seven,*
> *And all before daylight.'*

Now it so happened that about half a mile from the old farmhouse where Maisie stayed there was a beautiful castle where a very rich young nobleman lived. All the mothers who had pretty daughters used to wish that he would come their way some day and fall in love with one of them. He had never done so and it was said that he was too grand to marry any country girl and that one day he would cross the border and go away to London and marry a duke's daughter.

It chanced that this fine spring morning the young nobleman's favourite horse had lost a shoe and he was riding it on the soft grass on his way to the smithy. He was passing Maisie's garden gate when her mother came into the garden singing the strange lines. He stopped his horse and said, 'Good morning, madam, may I ask why you sing such a strange song?'

Maisie's mother did not answer but turned and walked into the house. The young nobleman, being very anxious to know what it all meant, hung his horse's bridle over the garden gate and followed her into the kitchen. She pointed to the seven hanks of thread lying on the table and said: 'This hath my daughter done before breakfast.'

The young man asked to see the girl who was so industrious. Her mother then went and pulled Maisie from behind the door where she had hidden herself after coming downstairs while her mother was in the garden. She looked so lovely in her fresh morning gown of blue gingham with her auburn hair curling softly round her brow and her face blushing all over at the sight of such a gallant young man, he in turn lost his heart and fell in love with her on the spot.

The young nobleman explained that his dear mother had always told him to try and find a wife who was both pretty and useful and that this morning he had succeeded beyond his expectations. He then proposed marriage and Maisie's mother was overjoyed.

Maisie herself was a little perplexed as she was afraid that she would be expected to spin a great deal when she was married and lived at the castle. If that were so, her husband was sure to find out that she was not really such a good spinstress as he thought she was.

In her trouble she went down, the night before her wedding, to the great boulder by the stream and climbing on it she laid her head against the stone and called softly down the hole: 'Habetrot, dear Habetrot.' The little old woman soon appeared and with a twinkle in her eyes she asked Maisie what was troubling her so much just when she should have been very happy about her marriage to the young nobleman. Maisie then told her. 'Trouble not your pretty head about that,' answered the fairy, 'but come here with your bridegroom next week when the moon is full and I warrant that he will never ask thee to sit at a spinning-wheel again.'

Accordingly, after all the wedding festivities were over and the couple had settled down at the castle, on the appointed evening Maisie suggested to her husband that they should take a walk together in the moon-light.

She was very anxious to see what the little fairy would do to help her for that very day her husband had been showing her all over her new home and he had pointed out to her a beautiful new spinning-wheel made of ebony which he said had belonged to his mother. He also told her that on the following day he would bring lint from the town and he was looking forward to seeing how clever she was at spinning. Maisie had blushed as red as a rose as she bent over the lovely wheel and then felt sick as she wondered what would happen if Habetrot was unable to help her.

So on this particular evening, after they had walked in the garden, Maisie said that she would like to go down to the little dell and see how the stream looked in the moonlight. So to the dell they went.

As soon as they came to the boulder Maisie put her head against it and whispered: 'Habetrot, dear Habetrot,' and in an instant the little woman appeared. She bowed in a stately way as if they were both strangers to her and said: 'Welcome, sir and madam, to the Spinsters' Dell.' She then tapped on the root of a great oak tree with a tiny wand which she held in her hand and a green door which Maisie never remembered having noticed before flew open and they followed the fairy through it into the other valley which Maisie had seen through the hole in the great stone.

All the little women were sitting on their white chucky stones busy at work, only they seemed far uglier than they had seemed at first and Maisie noticed that the reason for this was that instead of wearing red skirts and white mutches as they had done before, they now wore caps and dresses of dull grey. Instead of looking happy they all seemed to be trying to look miserable while they pushed their long lips out to wet their fingers to draw the thread from their distaffs.

'Save us and help us! What a lot of hideous old witches,' exclaimed the husband. 'Whatever could this funny old woman mean by bringing a pretty girl like you to look at them? You will dream of them for a week and a day. Just look at their lips.' Pushing Maisie behind him,

her husband went up to one of them and asked her what had made her mouth grow so ugly. She tried to tell him, but all the sound that he could hear was something that sounded like SPIN-N-N. He asked another one and her answer sounded like SPAN-N-N. He tried a third and her reply sounded like SPUN-N-N. He seized Maisie by the hand and hurried her through the green door.

'By my soul,' he said. 'My mother's spinning-wheel may turn to gold before I let you touch it if this is what spinning leads to. Rather than that your pretty face be spoiled the linen chests at the castle may get empty and remain so for ever.'

So it came to pass that Maisie could be out of doors all day wandering about with her husband and laughing and singing to her heart's content. Whenever there was lint at the castle to be spun it was carried down to the big boulder in the dell and left there. It was then collected by Habetrot and her companions who spun it for the linen chests and there was no more trouble about the matter.

The page boy and the silver goblet

There was once a little page boy who was in service in a stately castle on the Scottish west coast. He was a pleasant, good-natured little fellow and carried out his duties so willingly that he was popular with everyone including the great earl whom he served every day and the fat old butler for whom he ran errands. The castle stood on the edge of a cliff overlooking the sea and although the walls on that side were very thick there was a small postern door which allowed only one person to pass through to a narrow flight of steps cut out of the cliff side and leading down to the seashore. The shore was a pleasant place on summer mornings when one could bathe in the shimmering sea.

On the other side of the castle were gardens and pleasure grounds opening on to a long stretch of heather-covered moorland and beyond was a chain of lofty mountains. The little page boy was very fond of going out on the moor when his work was done. He could then run about as much as he liked, chasing bumblebees, catching butterflies and looking for birds' nests when it was nesting time and watching the young birds learning to fly.

The old butler was very pleased that he should go out on the moor for he knew that it was good for a healthy little lad to have plenty of fun in the open air. But before the boy went out the old man always gave him one warning. 'Now, mind my words, laddie, and keep away from the fairy knowe on the moor, for the little folk are not to be trusted.'

This knowe of which he spoke was a little green hillock which stood on the moor about fifty yards from the garden gate and the local people said that it was the abode of the fairies who would punish any rash mortal who went too near them. It was also known as Boot Hill and according to the great earl the hillock had been made hundreds of years before when visiting noblemen cleaned the earth and mud from their boots on the hill before entering the castle. Because of the various stories the country folk would walk a good half mile out of their way, even in broad daylight, rather than run the risk of going near the hillock and bringing the little folk's displeasure down upon themselves. At night, they said, the fairies walked abroad, leaving the door of their dwelling open so that any foolish mortal who did not take care might find himself inside.

Now, the little page boy was an adventurous lad, and instead of being frightened of the fairies he was very anxious to see them and visit their abode, just to find out what it was like. One night, when everyone else was asleep, he crept out of the castle by the little postern door and stole down the steps, then along the seashore to a path leading up on to the moor.

He went straight to the fairy knowe and to his delight he found that what the local people had said was true. The top of the knowe was tipped up and from the opening came rays of light streaming into the darkness. His heart was beating fast with excitement, but gathering his courage he stooped down and slipped inside. He found himself in a large room lit by numberless tiny candles and there, seated round a polished marble table, were scores of tiny folk; fairies, elves and gnomes, dressed in green, yellow, pink, blue, lilac and scarlet; in fact, all the colours of the rainbow.

The little page boy stood in a dark corner watching the busy scene in wonder, thinking how strange it was that there should be such a number of those tiny beings living their own lives all unknown to men and yet not far away from human dwellings. Suddenly an order was given by whom he could not tell.

'Fetch the cup,' cried the unknown voice and instantly two little fairy pages dressed in scarlet livery darted from the table to a cupboard in the wall of the compartment. They returned staggering under the weight of a most beautiful silver goblet, richly embossed and lined inside with gold.

The silver cup was placed on the middle of the table and, amid clapping of hands and shouts of joy, all the fairies began to drink out of it in turn. The page boy could see from where he stood that no one poured wine into the cup and yet it appeared to be always full. The wine that was in it was not always of the same kind, but sometimes red and sometimes white. Each fairy, when he grasped the stem, wished for the wine he desired, and lo, in a moment the cup was full of it. 'It would be a fine thing if I could take that cup home with me,' thought the page boy. 'No one will believe that I have been here unless I have something to show for it.' So he bided his time and waited.

Presently the fairies noticed him and, instead of being angry at his boldness in entering their abode, as he expected, they seemed very pleased to see him and invited him to take a seat at the table. But not long after he sat down they became rude and insolent, whispering together and peering at him and asking why he should be content to serve mere mortals. They also told him that they were aware of everything that went on in the castle and made fun about the old butler whom the page boy loved. They laughed at the food served in the castle and said it was only fit for animals. When any fresh, dainty food was set on the table by the scarlet-clad fairy pages they would

push the dish across to him saying: 'Taste it, for you will not have the chance to taste such good things at the castle.'

At last, he could stand their teasing remarks no longer; besides, he knew that if he wanted to secure the silver cup he must not lose any more time in doing so as they all appeared to be turning against him. Suddenly he stood up and grabbed the cup from the table, holding the stem of it lightly in his hand.

'I will drink to you all in water,' he cried, and instantly

the ruby-red wine in the cup was changed to clear, cold water. He raised the cup to his lips but did not drink from it. With a sudden jerk he threw the water over the burning candles and instantly the room was in darkness. Then, clasping the precious cup tightly in his arms, he sprang to the opening of the knowe through which he could see the stars gleaming clearly in the sky. He was just in time for the opening like a trap door fell with a crash behind him. Soon he was speeding along the moor with the whole troop of fairies at his heels. They were wild with rage and from the shrill shouts of fury the page boy knew that if they overtook him he could expect no mercy at their hands.

The page boy's heart began to sink, for fleet of foot though he was he was no match for the fairy folk who were steadily gaining on him. All seemed lost, when a mysterious voice sounded out of the darkness:

> *'If you would gain the castle door,*
> *Keep to the black stones on the shore.'*

It was the voice of some poor mortal, who, for some reason or other, had been taken prisoner by the fairies and who did not want such a fate to befall the adventurous page boy; but the little fellow did not know this. He had once heard that if one walked on the wet sands which the waves had washed over the fairies could not touch him. The mysterious voice brought the saying into his mind. He dashed panting down the path to the shore, his feet sank into the dry sand and his breath came in little gasps. He felt as if he must drop the silver cup and give up the struggle, but he persevered and at last, just as the foremost fairies were about to lay hands on him, he jumped across the water mark on to firm, wet sand from which the waves had just receded. He was now safe. The little folk could go no further but stood on the dry sand uttering cries of rage and disappointment while the page boy ran triumphantly by the edge of the sea carrying the precious cup in his arms. He climbed lightly up the steps in the rock and disappeared through the postern door into the castle.

For many years afterwards, long after the little page boy had grown up and had become a stately butler who trained other little page boys to follow in his footsteps, the beautiful goblet remained in the castle as a witness to his adventure.

Notes

The piper of Badenoch
The same story under the title 'The piper of Sutherland' appears in *Scottish Legendary Tales* by Elizabeth Sheppard-Jones, published by Thomas Nelson & Sons Ltd, Edinburgh and London (1962). At the end of March 1958, five soldiers of the Cameron Highlanders claimed to have heard the ghost-piper while on an exercise near Kingussie.

The seal-catcher
Taken from the story 'The seal-catcher and the merman' which appeared in *The Scottish Fairy Book* by Elizabeth W. Grierson, published by T. Fisher Unwin Ltd, London (1910 and 1915).

The meal mill of Eathie
Taken from the story of 'Tam McKechan' which appeared in *Scenes and Legends of the North of Scotland* by Hugh Miller, published by W. P. Nimmo, Hay and Mitchell, Edinburgh (1889). The same story under the title 'The mill at Eathie' also appears in *Scottish Legendary Tales* by Elizabeth Sheppard-Jones.

It is believed by some that Thomas McKechan returned from Fairyland seven years after his disappearance – but he did not return to Rosemarkie. This theory is supported by the fact that there was one Thomas McKechan executed at Perth for sheep-stealing just a few months after the seven-year time limit had expired.

The Laird o' Co
Traditional story, also from *The Scottish Fairy Book* by Elizabeth W. Grierson, London (1910).

The blacksmith and the fairies
Taken from the book *Scottish Fairy and Folk Tales* by Sir George Douglas (1896) and published some time before 1900 by the Walter Scott Publishing Company, London and Felling-on-Tyne, now out of print, but republished in 1977 by E. P. Publishing Ltd, East Ardsley, Wakefield, Yorks. The original tale of 'The blacksmith and the fairies' appeared in Campbell's *Popular Tales of the West Highlands*.

The fox and the wolf
This is the traditional story of the finding of the keg of butter, with the addition of two legends, i.e. the fox ridding himself of the fleas and the moon thought to be a cheese in the duck pond.

The elfin knight
From *The Scottish Fairy Book* by Elizabeth W. Grierson, London (1910).

The brownie and the green slippers
The Doune Hill and a Rothiemurchus Brownie are referred to in the notes to *Memoirs of a Highland Lady*, edited by Lady Strachey (1898). The same book refers to the *greusiach*, (shoemaker) attending once a week at the laird's house.

Thomas the Rhymer
Traditional tale, this version from *The Scottish Fairy Book* by Elizabeth W. Grierson, London (1910).

The Dwarfie Stone
Traditional, from *The Scottish Fairy Book* by Elizabeth W. Grierson, London (1910).

Habetrot the spinstress
Said to be a story from Selkirkshire, it is a parallel tale to 'The three spinners' by the brothers Grimm.

The page boy and the silver goblet
Traditional, from *The Scottish Fairy Book* by Elizabeth W.
Grierson, London (1910).

All these books are available at your local bookshop or newsagent, or can be ordered direct from the publisher. Indicate the number of copies required and fill in the form below.

Send to: **CS Department, Pan Books Ltd., P.O. Box 40, Basingstoke, Hants. RG21 2YT.**

or phone: 0256 469551 (Ansaphone), quoting title, author and Credit Card number.

Please enclose a remittance* to the value of the cover price plus: 60p for the first book plus 30p per copy for each additional book ordered to a maximum charge of £2.40 to cover postage and packing.

*Payment may be made in sterling by UK personal cheque, postal order, sterling draft or international money order, made payable to Pan Books Ltd.

Alternatively by Barclaycard/Access:

Card No.

Signature:

Applicable only in the UK and Republic of Ireland.

While every effort is made to keep prices low, it is sometimes necessary to increase prices at short notice. Pan Books reserve the right to show on covers and charge new retail prices which may differ from those advertised in the text or elsewhere.

NAME AND ADDRESS IN BLOCK LETTERS PLEASE:

Name

Address